william Maxwell

Littlenose and the Bear Hunt

Littlenose is bored. There is nothing to do and he is tired of playing with Two-Eyes, his pet mammoth. So he heads down to the river in search of new ideas – and there he hears some strange noises. Creeping up, he spies a family of otters playing on a mud slide – and immediately realises what a wonderful time he could have on a boy-sized mud slide! But what Littlenose doesn't know is that someone is spying on him – and they're not playing . . .

For Lucy and Hannah

# Littlenose and the Bear Hunt

John Grant

**KNIGHT BOOKS**
Hodder and Stoughton

Printed and bound in Great Britain for
Hodder and Stoughton Paperbacks, a divi-
sion of Hodder and Stoughton Ltd, Mill
Road, Dunton Green, Sevenoaks, Kent
TN13 2YA (Editorial Office: 47 Bedford
Square, London WC1B 3DP) by Clays
Ltd, St Ives plc. Photoset by Rowland
Phototypesetting Ltd, Bury St Edmunds,
Suffolk.

A Catalogue record for this book is avail-
able from the British Library

ISBN 0-340-57947-1

# Contents

# Chapter One

## Littlenose is Bored

It was a bright, warm, sunny morning. At least, it was as warm as it ever was during the Ice Age, thousands of years ago. Among the caves of the Neanderthal Folk there was the usual morning bustle. Hunters set off with their spears. Others went into the woods to gather firewood. Others again trudged up from the river with clay pots of

fresh water. Everyone was smiling and cheerful on such a fine morning. Except Littlenose. He sat by the entrance to his family cave, scuffed his feet in the dust, and wrinkled his berry-sized nose which gave him his name. The rest of the Neanderthal Folk had big, red, snuffly noses of which they were very proud.

8

Father came out of the cave carrying his hunt-ing spear. He tripped on Littlenose's out-stretched legs and shouted, 'Have you nothing better to do than sit there getting in everyone's way?'

'I've nothing to do,' said Littlenose. 'I'm bored.'

Father grunted, and went on his way. Little-nose stood up and wandered into the cave. Mother was clearing up after breakfast. Little-nose ambled about picking things up and putting them down. After she had bumped into him twice, she shouted, 'Stop dithering about! Go outside and do something! Go and play with Two-Eyes!' Two-Eyes was Littlenose's pet mammoth.

'I can't think what to do,' said Littlenose. 'And I'm tired of playing with Two-Eyes. I'm bored.'

'What about your chores?' said Mother.

'Done them,' said Littlenose. 'Fetched water. Chopped sticks. Made my bed. I've nothing left to do. That's why I'm bored.'

Father came back into the cave. He had forgotten something.

'Littlenose is bored,' said Mother.

'Look at Two-Eyes,' said Father. 'He doesn't look bored. Animals never get bored. Nor birds. They're always busy about something or other. They are an example to us all.' And he went out again, muttering about today's children and how *he* was never bored when he was Littlenose's age.

Littlenose sighed, and started to fidget. But Mother gave him one of her looks and he went outside. Two-Eyes followed.

A bird was singing in a nearby tree.

'That's it,' thought Littlenose, 'I'll sing a song. It will cheer me up, and the others will be glad of a spot of music.' He sat down on a handy rock, took a deep breath, and started to sing. He wasn't sure of all the words. And there were parts of the tune he had forgotten, but he filled in with 'dum-de-dums' here and there.

And it began to make him feel much more

cheerful. But he was the only one! Heads popped out of caves. And Mother shouted, 'Stop that dreadful noise, Littlenose. What on earth will the neighbours think?'

Littlenose knew exactly what the neighbours thought. They shouted at him even more loudly than Mother, and they threw old pieces of bone and fish heads and even more unpleasant things at Littlenose.

'There's no pleasing some people,' he thought. He went down to the river. He might get some ideas there.

But he didn't. At least, not to begin with.

Then, a frog came hopping through the grass. It stopped by Littlenose's feet. He stooped down for a closer look, and the frog took two long hops, and vanished with a plop into the river. Through the clear water he watched it swimming until it disappeared.

'Hopping,' thought Littlenose. 'That might be fun.'

He crouched down, then hopped forward just as he had seen the frog do. It wasn't easy, but Littlenose was not one to give up. Until he tripped on a tree root and sprawled with a bump on the hard ground. 'Not a lot of fun in that,' he thought, 'unless, of course, you're a frog!'

Out in the middle of the river a large fish suddenly leapt high out of the water. Now, *that* could be fun! The fish landed with a loud splash, and Littlenose had to admit that there was a problem. He couldn't swim! None of the Neanderthal Folk could swim. They hadn't learned. They hadn't even tried. The Neanderthal Folk thought that being able to swim was, like a lot of other things, not quite respectable. Actually, Littlenose's Uncle Redhead could swim, but nobody thought that Uncle Redhead was respectable anyway.

Littlenose made his way further along the bank of the river. The woods came right to the top of the bank, which was as tall as Littlenose. He still hadn't thought of anything to do, and walked along, head down, thinking hard.

And then he heard a noise. Every Neanderthal child was taught that noises, particularly in the woods, could mean danger. Littlenose looked for a tree to climb!

But the noises didn't sound very dangerous. Not growling. Nor roaring like a hungry bear or sabre tooth tiger. There was a lot of squeaking and squealing. It was really a very happy sort of noise. It came from the river bank, beyond the trees.

Littlenose crept forward. He pushed his way
through the bushes and some way along the bank
he saw a wonderful sight: a family of otters at
play. The bank was wet and muddy, and the
otters were climbing to the top and sliding back
down into the water. Two grown-up otters and
three young ones rolled, tumbled and slid down
the muddy bank with much chattering and
squeaking which Littlenose guessed was otter
laughter. It was very exciting. So exciting that
Littlenose jumped to his feet and clapped his
hands with delight.

In a flash the otters were gone! There was barely a ripple on the river to show where they had been. But Littlenose had almost forgotten the otters already. A wonderful idea was forming in his mind. A mud slide! Not an otter-size one, but a boy-size mud slide! No one could possibly be bored with a mud slide to play on!

It must be almost lunch time. In the afternoon he would come back to the river bank and find a good mud slide place. The rest would be easy.

## Chapter Two

# Mud and Black Bears

Mother was very relieved when Littlenose arrived home for lunch smiling broadly.

'You're not bored any more!' she exclaimed.

'No,' said Littlenose. 'What's for lunch?'

'Your favourite,' said Mother. 'Rhinoceros soup.'

Littlenose sat down and began gulping down the soup as fast as he could.

'Take your time!' cried Mother. 'How often do you have to be told to eat more slowly?'

Littlenose finished his soup.

'More?' asked Mother.

Littlenose shook his head. 'No thank you. I've got a busy afternoon ahead of me,' he said, and hurried out of the cave. Father had been too busy eating to speak. He looked up. 'That boy's sickening for something. Not waiting for a second helping! Very odd!'

'At least he isn't bored,' said Mother. Father only grunted.

Meanwhile Littlenose was hurrying through the woods towards the river.

He had to find a really good place for his mud slide. Somewhere where the river bank was high, not too steep, and muddy.

It was difficult to see the bank from among the trees, so Littlenose pushed through the bushes and climbed down to the water's edge. He walked along, sometimes wading in the water, and looking all the time for a piece of bank that was the right height and not covered in bushes and weeds. Several times he climbed up the bank for a closer look. The afternoon slipped by, and Littlenose was hot, tired, and covered in earth and mud.

Then, he found it. Rain had washed away the grass and bushes. Smooth, bare clay went right to the top, many times taller than Littlenose. He scrambled up to the top. It was just right . . .

except for one thing. It was dry! It wasn't slippery at all. Littlenose could stand quite comfortably on the dry clay. Perhaps it would be fine after a shower of rain. He looked up at the sky. There wasn't a single rain cloud. But it was time to set off for home. He would think about the problem on the way.

Littlenose had only gone a short distance when something made him stop. It was a noise. But not a happy noise like the otters made. This was very definitely a *hungry* noise, and getting closer by the moment. Littlenose looked around for a tree to climb, but the nearest were spindly saplings. He started to run, and the hungry noises were now not only getting louder, but were accompanied by heavy footsteps crunching through the undergrowth. Littlenose raced

across a clearing. On the far side was a tall tree with thick, bushy foliage. Up he went as fast as he could climb. Lying along a stout branch, Littlenose peered through the leaves to the ground below.

Out from among the trees on the far side of the clearing came an enormous black bear with her two cubs. The three bears stood sniffing the air. They looked this way and that. They rose up on their hind legs to see better. But there was still no sign of the Neanderthal boy they had been looking forward to eating. Fresh Neanderthal child was a favourite meal for black bears. The cubs sat down and howled with disappointment until the she-bear cuffed them and growled at them to be quiet.

Up in his tree, Littlenose quaked with terror. He knew that bears were very good at climbing trees. If they thought to follow his scent across the clearing to the foot of the tree he was lost. He looked about him. His tree was not too far from another just as big. Indeed, one of the branches leaned right across almost touching a branch of the other tree. Littlenose began to inch his way towards the trunk, then out along in the direction of the second tree.

Now the mother bear had her nose to the ground. With the cubs yelping excitedly behind her she snuffled her way to the foot of Littlenose's tree. Then she stood upright and peered up into the branches. The Neanderthal boy must be up there. There was no other place for him to go!

But Littlenose was already pulling himself quietly along into the foliage of the other tree. The branch he was on was covered in damp moss. His hands, arms and body were soon smeared with green, as well as with the mud from the river bank. But now he had reached the trunk. On the side furthest from the clearing and the bears he dropped quietly into the long grass . . . and ran like the wind for home and safety.

The bears waited until sunset, then returned to their den in disgust.

Mother was just about to serve the evening meal when Littlenose walked into the cave. She took one look at him and shrieked, 'Outside, this minute! You are not coming into my clean cave like that!'

Father looked up. 'Yes! Outside! And take those filthy furs off! You don't see me coming in covered in dirt from head to foot . . . even after a hard day's hunting!'

Littlenose took off his furs. Then Father came out of the cave carrying Mother's largest clay bowl. It was filled with water, and Father tipped it over Littlenose. He handed him an old scrap of fur, and Littlenose scrubbed and scraped at the mud and moss. Twice more Father tipped a bowlful of water over him. Then he made him stand by the fire to get dry, because, of course, there were no towels in those days! When he was dry, Mother handed him a clean pair of furs, and he sat down to eat.

'Let's have no more of this nonsense,' said Father. 'If I can come home at the end of the day clean and tidy, there is no reason why you can't.'

But Littlenose wasn't even listening. While he had been standing under the water that Father poured from the clay bowl, he had had a wonderful idea. He knew how he was going to make his mud slide. He would start first thing after breakfast.

# Chapter Three

## A Clay Pot and Water

As soon as Littlenose woke next morning he remembered his wonderful idea. He would borrow one of Mother's large clay pots and use it to carry river water to make his mud slide really slippery. He decided not to ask for the loan of a pot. It was much easier simply borrowing one! After breakfast, he waited until Father had gone to a hunters' meeting, and Mother had gone to pay a call on a sick neighbour. Then he began rummaging in the corner of the cave where Mother kept her cooking utensils. There were several which she used every day, but Littlenose realised that she was likely to miss one of those and make a fuss about it. He found what he was looking for. Right at the back of the heap was a large clay pot. It was dusty. It was chipped in places around the rim. It didn't look as if it had been used for a very long time.

Checking to make sure that the coast was clear, Littlenose made to get the pot out of the cave. It was much heavier than he had expected. He carried it to the entrance, and put in down, his arms aching. He carried it another few steps before he had to stop to rest again. This was ridiculous. He would be *weeks* just getting to the mud slide, let alone carrying water from the river to the top of the bank.

Two-Eyes came ambling up, wondering what Littlenose was up to this time. 'Come on, Two-Eyes!' shouted Littlenose. 'This is where you can help. Wait here!' He ran back into the cave, while Two-Eyes stood wondering why he didn't just run away. Littlenose was up to something, and that usually meant trouble for someone . . . frequently Two-Eyes. Littlenose reappeared

with a coil of Father's raw-hide rope. He heaved
the clay pot on to Two-Eyes' back. Then he tied
it tight with the rope. 'Off we go, Two-Eyes!' he
said.

Littlenose hurried ahead. He was impatient to get to work. But Two-Eyes lagged behind. 'Hurry up!' shouted Littlenose.

'Hm! It's all very well for him!' said Two-Eyes to himself in mammoth language. '*He's* not carrying an enormous pot on his back.' And, what was worse, Littlenose's knots were working loose. The pot didn't fall off, but it slid suddenly to one side, and Two-Eyes fell over with a thump!

'Oh! stop messing about!' shouted Littlenose. But he hurried back and helped the little mammoth to his feet. Then he tightened the rope, and they went on their way again.

To Two-Eyes' great relief it was not long before Littlenose cried, 'Here we are. This is the place.' He took the clay pot from Two-Eyes' back. Two-Eyes found a shady spot, lay down, and fell asleep. Littlenose, however, had work to do. He dragged the pot to the edge of the bank. Then, holding it as carefully as he could, he slid and slithered down to the river's edge. Filling it with water was easy. Lifting it up and tipping the water on to the clay bank wasn't quite so easy. In fact, it was quite difficult. It got even more difficult as Littlenose worked higher and higher up the bank. It also took a lot of water. The ground soaked it up almost faster than Littlenose poured it. He paused for a rest and looked up. This was going to take for ever. Then he had another of his wonderful ideas: Two-Eyes could help.

Two-Eyes wasn't pleased at being roused and having one end of the rope tied around him. Littlenose threw the other end to the foot of the bank. Then he slid down after it and tied it securely to the pot. 'When I shout "PULL",

Two-Eyes,' he called, 'pull as hard as you can!'

Two-Eyes muttered to himself. He was fed up with the whole affair, and he was also uneasy. He waved his trunk and sniffed the air. There was something not quite right!

Hidden in the undergrowth, three pairs of eyes
watched Littlenose and Two-Eyes. The she-bear
and her cubs had heard the noise, and now they
could hardly believe their eyes. Not just a tender
Neanderthal boy, but a plump young mammoth
as well. They waited for just the right moment
while Littlenose filled the pot with water, and
shouted to Two-Eyes to pull. Littlenose quickly
climbed up to join him. He took hold of the rope
and together they dragged the heavy pot to the
top. Except that it was not as heavy as it ought to
have been. It was nearly empty! The last trickle
of water was disappearing through a large crack
in the bottom. No wonder Mother didn't use it.
The dirt must have hidden the crack, and the

water had washed it away. Littlenose had spilt so much water to begin with that he didn't notice that the pot was leaking. He almost wept with vexation.

The bears were now very close. Hidden by the river bank, they crept up, licking their lips.

Littlenose untied the useless pot. He gave it a push with his foot, so that it rolled over the edge. The bears looked up as something hurtled down upon them. It hit the ground and burst into a hundred pieces with a loud crash. Panic-stricken, the bears fled!

Not even knowing that he had come close to becoming a bears' dinner, Littlenose heaved a great sigh. Everything was going wrong. He was never going to have his mud slide. Two-Eyes wasn't interested in mud slides, but he didn't like to see Littlenose unhappy. His sharp mammoth ears had picked up an interesting sound. He listened for a moment, then he got up and went off by himself.

Two-Eyes had heard a different sound of running water – not only the river, but a small stream flowing into it. Two-Eyes found the stream. He dipped his trunk into the water and sucked up as much as he could, and hurried back to Littlenose.

Littlenose watched in surprise as Two-Eyes trotted to the edge of the river bank and squirted the water out of his trunk. He went back to the stream for more. And more again. Littlenose clapped his hands. 'What a clever mammoth you are!' he cried. 'I'll help you!' Littlenose hadn't a trunk, but he took a big mouthful of water. Unfortunately, he tripped on a root and swallowed most of it. He decided that it was better to leave Two-Eyes to get on with it. And soon there was a wonderfully wet and slippery slope all the way from the top of the bank to the foot.

Littlenose reckoned that this must surely be the best mud slide ever. But, of course, the only way to find out was to try it.

But it was getting late. He ought to be getting off home. Yes, he would wait until tomorrow, then he could spend all day on the slide, not just a few minutes. He called to Two-Eyes. Together they set off for the cave.

And the bears? They sat in their den, hungry and fed-up. But they were not going to give up. Neanderthal boy and mammoth were worth waiting for.

# Chapter Four

## Father and Firewood

Tomorrow came with a rather nasty surprise for Littlenose. Father woke him early. 'Come on,' he said. 'Time to get up. There's work to be done!'

'How did *he* know,' thought Littlenose, 'that I was going to try out my mud slide?'

But Father didn't know. He was talking about something completely different. He and Littlenose were going into the woods to collect firewood. Littlenose started to protest, but Father silenced him with a look. Mother had breakfast ready. Littlenose looked out of the cave. The morning was grey and cold-looking. There had been heavy rain in the night. 'Just the thing to make my mud slide extra slippery,' he thought to himself.

'Two-Eyes had better come,' said Father. 'He can carry the firewood.'

Two-Eyes muttered a mammoth mutter to himself. 'I'd be twice the height I am if they didn't keep putting heavy loads on me! First clay pots! Now firewood!'

'Right! Off we go!' said Father, leading the way. And he set off, axe in hand, with Littlenose and Two-Eyes trudging behind. They took the same path as Littlenose and Two-Eyes had done

the day before. They passed the place where the
otters had their mud slide. 'Lucky them,' Littlenose whispered to Two-Eyes. 'I bet no one
ever makes *them* gather firewood instead of having fun.'

When it seemed that they had been walking for
ever, Father said, 'Here we are.' A dead tree had
blown down not long before. The dry branches
made excellent firewood. Green wood filled the
cave with smoke, but dry, dead wood burned
with a bright flame and cooked food quickly, as
well as keeping people warm. Father spat on his
hands and took a firm grip of his stone axe. Then

he started chopping. Littlenose's job was to collect the chopped wood and make it into bundles. With his flint knife he cut strips of bark and used them to tie the bundles. Two-Eyes lay down for a nap. When Father decided that they had enough bundles of firewood, they would be loaded on to his back for the long journey back home.

While Father chopped, Littlenose tied, and Two-Eyes dozed, the sound of the axe had not gone unnoticed!

The she-bear and her cubs were sitting outside their den. Game was scarce, and a breakfast of three frogs and two snails among them made them as bad-tempered as bears with sore heads

. . . or rather bears with empty stomachs!

But the sound of voices, and the clunking of a stone axe, made them sit up. Twice they had almost enjoyed fresh Neanderthal boy. The third time might just be lucky!

Followed by her cubs, the mother bear walked cautiously in the direction of the sounds. The voices were no further away than the other side of a clump of bushes. With nose and paws the bear pushed aside the leaves. Littlenose had tied up the last bundle of wood, and Father was securing it on Two-Eyes' back.

The bear opened her eyes wide in astonishment. Neanderthal boy! Mammoth! And an old Neanderthal! Probably a bit tough, that one, but hungry bears couldn't be too fussy. She growled very softly to the cubs to get ready to follow her. Neither Father nor Littlenose heard the growl, but Two-Eyes' sharp mammoth ears heard it. With a terrified squeal, he fled as fast as he could into the trees. Littlenose ran after him. 'Come back, Two-Eyes!' he shouted. 'What's the matter with you?'

Father picked up his axe. 'Stupid animal!' he exclaimed. 'Every bit as daft as Littlenose!'

And, at that moment, the bears charged out of the bushes.

Father yelled even louder than Two-Eyes. Then, he ran like the wind.

And so did the bears!

Father dodged round trees. Leapt over rocks. Crashed through bushes. And the bears kept coming. They weren't getting any closer. But they were no further away.

'Littlenose!' shouted Father as he ran. 'Where are you? Do something!'

Littlenose was clinging to a slender branch high above the ground. Two-Eyes cowered in a briar thicket. They both heard Father. And they heard the bears, which were beginning to growl happily at the thought of the meal to come.

'Over this way!' cried Littlenose. But his voice echoed among the trees of the wood, and Father had no idea where it was coming from. He dashed this way and that, while the three bears got closer by the moment. Then, with a snapping and crackling of twigs, something came rushing through the undergrowth. Two-Eyes had decided to do something. He wasn't sure what, but Father was in trouble. That was enough. He raised his small trunk and trumpeted as he charged. And at that moment the rope holding the load of firewood broke. In the shadows of the undergrowth the bears saw something bulky which bounced and rolled on the ground. They dived on it with jaws wide. They spat out pieces of twig and bark and looked around for Father once more.

But Father was gone, running fast still, while Littlenose shouted encouragement from his tree-top. Father was running close to the high river bank. He was heading for a gap in the bushes. Littlenose caught a glimpse of him. 'No! Not

that way! Over here!' he shouted. But Father didn't hear, or wasn't listening. The bears were still on his trail. He burst through the gap . . . and on to Littlenose's mud slide!

With a yell, he vanished over the edge!

# Chapter Five

## Father has a Slide

For a moment, Father kept his feet. Then he fell back with a squelch on the mud, and rolled, slid and slithered down the steep bank. He landed in the shallow water with a splash just as the bears reached the top of the bank. The mother bear gave a loud growl and leapt over the edge.

*She* didn't keep her feet. Her legs shot in all directions. On her stomach she slid down head first. The mud splashed up her nose and into her eyes. Then she was in the river, a large and very confused ball of muddy fur! The cubs watched from the top. Their mother wiped the mud from her eyes and blew it from her nose. Where was the old Neanderthal they were hunting?

Father, the old Neanderthal, was nowhere to be seen. Before the bear set foot on Littlenose's mud slide he was already running fast, splashing through the shallow water. Littlenose called, 'This way, Father! The bank is low! You can climb up here!'

The bear pricked up her ears at the sound of Littlenose's voice. She rose on her hind legs to sniff the air . . . and next moment she was knocked flying! The cubs, rushing to join their mother in the hunt for the old Neanderthal, had come down the mud slide behind her. Roaring with rage, she slapped and cuffed them with her enormous paws. Roaring, yelping, crying, the

three bears squabbled and tumbled over each other at the foot of the mud slide while out of sight Father scrambled up from the river to join Littlenose and Two-Eyes in the woods. By the time the bears calmed down, Father and Littlenose and Two-Eyes were out of sight and out of hearing of the bears.

They sat down in a clearing to get their breath back and decide what to do next. Father was covered in mud. He started scraping at it with a handful of grass, but it was dried hard. He found a puddle of rainwater, but that only smeared the mud and made it worse.

'What about the firewood?' asked Littlenose. 'After all, that's what we came for. And now it's lost. And I don't think we have time to find more before dark. And . . .'

But Father interrupted him. 'Don't chatter!' he exclaimed. 'I've enough problems without listening to you nattering away!'

'We can't go home without the firewood, Two-Eyes,' said Littlenose. 'Let's see if we can find it. Perhaps you can remember where it was it fell off your back. We'll just have to be very careful in case the bears are still about.'

But the bears, still hungry, were already on their way back to their den. Frogs and snails were perhaps not much to a hungry bear, but they were a lot less bother than Neanderthal boy, old Neanderthal, and mammoth!

It wasn't long before Littlenose spotted the bundles of firewood where they had fallen from Two-Eyes' back. 'Here we are!' he cried. 'Soon get you loaded up and on our way, Two-Eyes.'

Two-Eyes just went, 'Hmph!' He was rather hoping they would just forget all about the firewood.

They went back to where they had left Father. He was still scrubbing at the mud with handfuls of grass and leaves. 'How do I look?' he asked.

'Terrible!' said Littlenose. The mud had dried, and where Father had rubbed on the water from the puddle it was smeared. Grass and leaves were stuck all over him, particularly in his hair and beard. 'We should be on our way,' went on Littlenose. 'It's almost supper time. I wonder what we're having. I'm hungry.' And he set off with Two-Eyes, leaving Father to follow.

Mother saw Littlenose and Two-Eyes approaching the cave. She came out and said, 'What a fine lot of firewood. Oh, by the way, where's Father?'

'He'll be here shortly,' said Littlenose, beginning to unload the wood from Two-Eyes' back. Mother helped him carry it into the cave. She went outside for one last bundle. And screamed. She had caught sight of Father! 'What happened?' she cried.

'It's a long story,' said Littlenose.

'Yes,' said Father. 'And I haven't time to go into it now. I'm tired. I'm sore. And I'm very hungry. Just bring me my supper and don't ask questions!' And he made to go inside.

But Mother stood in the entrance with her hands on her hips. 'No, you don't,' she shouted, giving Father one of her looks. 'Stay outside! You are *not* coming into my clean cave like that! Take those filthy furs off! Littlenose, fetch a bowl of clean water . . . a large one!'

And poor Father had to stand outside while Littlenose and Mother poured water over him. It took a long time, but at last he was clean. Littlenose thought that it was all very amusing. He wanted to laugh, but he saw the expression on Father's face and decided he would laugh later, when Father wasn't there to hear him.

Dry, and wearing clean furs, Father sat down with Mother and Littlenose to a delicious supper. 'You're very quiet, Littlenose. What are you thinking?' asked Mother.

'Nothing, really,' said Littlenose. But he was thinking that perhaps the whole mud slide idea wasn't such a good one after all. But tomorrow was another day. He had plenty of time to think up something else to do.